# CONTENTS

KT-494-784

When the champions of Earth came together to battle a threat too big for a single hero, they realized the value of strength in numbers. Together they formed an unstoppable team, dedicated to defending the planet from the forces of evil. They are the . . .

{ ROLL CALL }

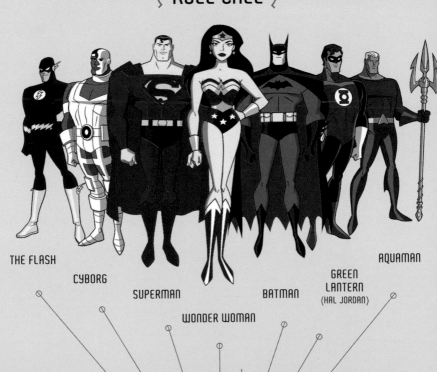

THE FLASH

CYBORG

SUPERMAN

WONDER WOMAN

BATMAN

GREEN
LANTERN
(HAL JORDAN)

AQUAMAN

# JUSTICE LEAGUE

## DARKSEID
### AND THE
## FIRES OF APOKOLIPS

BY
DEREK FRIDOLFS

ILLUSTRATED BY
TIM LEVINS

 raintree
a Capstone company — publishers for children

Published by Raintree, an imprint of Capstone Global Library Limited,
a company incorporated in England and Wales having its registered
office at 264 Banbury Road, Oxford, OX2 7DY – Registered company
number: 6695582

www.raintree.co.uk
myorders@raintree.co.uk

STAR39862

ISBN 978 1 4747 4904 6
21 20 19 18 17
10 9 8 7 6 5 4 3 2 1

A full catalogue record for this book is available from the British Library.

Editor: Christopher Harbo
Designer: Bob Lentz

Printed and bound in China.

MARTIAN
MANHUNTER

HAWKGIRL

HAWKMAN

GREEN ARROW

BLACK CANARY

GREEN LANTERN
(JOHN STEWART)

THE ATOM

SUPERGIRL

RED TORNADO

POWER GIRL

SHAZAM

PLASTIC MAN

BOOSTER GOLD

BLUE BEETLE

ZATANNA

VIXEN

METAMORPHO

ETRIGAN
THE DEMON

FIRESTORM

HUNTRESS

# CHAPTER 1

# BREAK IN

***KRUNNCH!***

Kalibak landed on a car parked along a street in Gotham City, breaking his fall. The hulking son of the super-villain Darkseid had jumped out of a window of the apartment above. Broken shards of glass rained down around him, sticking in his black beard and bouncing off his green uniform. People standing nearby ran for cover.

Crawling off the smashed vehicle, Kalibak slung a long, cylindrical case over his shoulder. Wary of his surroundings, he looked around to see if anyone noticed him.

Someone had.

"Whatever you just stole, I'll have to ask you to give it back," said Superman, his cape blowing around him.

The Man of Steel stood before Kalibak, blocking his path. Batman, Wonder Woman and The Flash soon arrived alongside him.

"You don't get to tell me what to do, Kryptonian!" sneered Kalibak. "Be careful what you wish for."

Kalibak removed the case from his back and opened it. Batman watched as the villain pulled out a long, ornate sword. As Kalibak tossed the weapon from hand to hand, Batman removed a Batarang from his Utility Belt just in case he needed it.

"Put the weapon down, Kalibak! You can't harm me with that," warned Superman.

A smile crept across Kalibak's rugged face. "Think again."

The blade of Kalibak's sword began glowing brightly. Batman drew up his cape to protect his vision. Wonder Woman used her bracelets to reflect the light. And The Flash closed his eyes to avoid its glare. But Superman wasn't so lucky.

Even squinting, the light blinded the Man of Steel. His vision blurred and went fuzzy. As the effects coursed through his body, his legs wobbled and he lost his balance. Kalibak used the opportunity to attack.

"Look out!" yelled Wonder Woman.

Charging forward with thunderous footsteps, Kalibak swung his sword at Superman. But Batman stepped in, tackling the Man of Steel out of the way as the sword sliced a parked car in half.

### SKRANNGG!

Superman crouched on the ground and blinked his eyes. His vision slowly returned. With his arm around Batman's shoulder, he struggled back to his feet.

"What just happened?" asked the Man of Steel. "Why did that weapon affect me?"

"It's not a normal sword, but one forged by magic," Batman answered. He knew Superman had a weakness to items of a magical nature. "I recognized it the moment Kalibak pulled it out. It's Excalibur!"

"King Arthur's sword? I thought it was a myth. How do you know?" asked Superman.

"Because I gave it as a gift to a close friend," answered the Dark Knight.

"That's some friend! I normally only get gift cards," The Flash said with a wink.

"Talk later," Wonder Woman said, nodding towards Kalibak. "Fight now!"

Reaching into his Utility Belt, Batman removed a round object and threw it towards Kalibak. **FSSSHHH!** The smoke grenade exploded, creating a thick cloud around him. But the smoke bomb barely provided cover. Kalibak simply walked through it.

"You'll have to do better than that, human!" he said.

Reaching for his Utility Belt, Batman gripped a bolo. The rope had two heavy metal balls at each end that could entangle almost any enemy.

The Dark Knight whipped the weapon towards Kalibak. The villain's large size prevented him from dodging, and the rope wrapped around his huge body. But it didn't hold him for long.

Kalibak used Excalibur's sharp blade to slash through the rope like butter. A wide, toothy smile stretched across the villain's face. Batman met it with a punch.

**KRAK!**

"You dare hit me, puny one!" yelled Kalibak in outrage.

Before the villain uttered a second insult, Batman punched Kalibak's midsection. Like a boxer, he landed rapid jabs to the villain's pressure points. The Dark Knight knew he couldn't keep up his attack for long. But he hoped he might have just enough strength to knock Kalibak out for the count. Instead, he left himself open for attack.

With his two large fists, Kalibak snagged Batman by his long, leathery cape. He swung him in a wide circle before releasing the Caped Crusader.

**CRIKK!** Batman crashed into a nearby building with enough force to crack the wall and send bricks flying.

"Be careful," warned Batman, leaning against the wall to push himself back to his feet. "Keep your distance from him."

"That's good advice. Why didn't you try it?" said Wonder Woman with a smile.

"Maybe if I'm quick enough, I won't have to," said The Flash. He dashed towards Kalibak to stop him.

With paper debris floating up into the air around him, The Flash circled Kalibak's body in a blur of red motion. Kalibak swung his sword over and over, but The Flash dodged before it could connect each time.

"Foolish insect," spat Kalibak, winded and annoyed. "Stay still so I can swat you!"

The Flash stopped directly in front of Kalibak, catching him by surprise. "What's the matter?" the Scarlet Speedster teased. "Am I *bugging* you?"

The Flash grabbed the sword with both hands to wrestle it free, but Kalibak had the tighter grip. The sword wouldn't budge.

Kalibak backhanded The Flash, knocking him end over end. His body bounced across the pavement before coming to a stop against a tree. Kalibak raised the sword directly over The Flash and slashed downwards.

### *CLANGG!*

A shower of sparks erupted as metal clashed against metal. Wonder Woman's bracelets intercepted the sword, locking it in place as she stood over The Flash to protect him.

"You are no match for the power of this sword!" boasted Kalibak. He applied his full weight to the sword. Wonder Woman fell to one knee, struggling to fend him off.

"She can't hold him back forever," warned Batman.

Using his heat vision, Superman shot lasers towards Kalibak. They struck his green uniform, but he stood unfazed.

"While he holds the sword, the magic of Excalibur protects him," said Batman.

"How can we stop him?" cried Superman.

Batman raised an eyebrow. "You can do more than use your eyes, can't you?"

**WHOOSH!**

Superman unleashed his super breath. A gale force wind lifted Kalibak off his feet. He tumbled down the street.

"Yes!" exclaimed The Flash. "You sent him *Kalibackwards!*"

Shaking off the cobwebs, Kalibak removed a remote control from his belt.

"You have been nothing more than a distraction," boasted Kalibak. "You're lucky I have lost interest." Then he pushed a button on the device and a large, circular doorway of light opened up around him. Before the members of the Justice League could react, he walked inside and disappeared.

*SHOOOM!*

"What now?" asked Wonder Woman as The Flash stood up beside her.

"We go and see the person who owned that sword," said Batman. He looked up at the broken window in the apartment above. "Someone I know personally."

With a swish of his cape, Batman entered the apartment building. His friends followed him up five flights of stairs before coming to a complete stop. The apartment's door was wide open, broken off its hinges. Within the apartment, furniture had been turned over, broken picture frames lay scattered on the floor and bookshelves stood empty.

"Looks like your friend could use a cleaner," said The Flash. "Who lives here?"

"Jason Blood," said Batman. "He's a collector of rare items."

"Well he won't be collecting the cleaning deposit," said The Flash. Batman threw him a sideways glance.

"This apartment used to house one of the greatest collections of artefacts related to the wizard Merlin," stated Batman. "Excalibur was one of many magical items Jason owned."

"Collecting football stickers and comics wasn't exciting enough?" asked The Flash.

"Jason collected these items for good reason," said Batman. "He's had a long history of being cursed."

"Like bad luck from broken mirrors?" asked The Flash.

"Worse," said Batman, picking up a picture frame. "Jason has lived a long life. Many years ago, Merlin the magician cursed Jason and forced him to share his body with the Demon Etrigan. The words of a magic spell could transform him into the Demon."

Batman paused to choose his next words carefully. "But once unleashed, Etrigan was hard to control. Jason has kept the Demon in check for a while, but he's spent lifetimes trying to safely separate himself from Etrigan. So far, he has been unsuccessful."

"Why *did* Jason keep Merlin's cursed objects here?" asked Superman.

"To keep them safe from prying eyes," said Batman. "So others wouldn't be hurt by Merlin's curses."

"Until now," said Wonder Woman, scanning the room. "It looks like they stole everything."

"And more importantly, where is Jason?" asked Superman.

"That's my cue. I've got this!" said The Flash with a smile.

**WHOOOSH!**

The Flash zoomed out of the room, kicking up dust and scraps of paper in his wake. Within seconds, he raced up and down staircases, checked rooms and searched the buildings in the surrounding city blocks.

## BA-BOOM!

A sonic shock wave announced The Flash's return to the apartment only moments later. Superman and Batman's capes fluttered in the breeze.

"He doesn't appear to be anywhere in this immediate area," The Flash reported. "And believe me – I've looked."

"I can't find him with my X-ray vision either," said Superman, looking through the walls of the apartment.

As Wonder Woman bent down to lift up an overturned chair, Batman spotted something.

The Dark Knight crouched down on the floor. He slid his fingers across the base of the chair to inspect it. It was the chair Jason Blood normally sat in.

"What is it?" asked Wonder Woman.

"There are claw marks here," answered Batman. "Maybe it's nothing, but it's worth investigating further." Using tweezers and a small paper envelope, he collected a wood sample from the damaged chair. He tucked the evidence securely inside a pouch in his Utility Belt.

"You've already got a theory, haven't you?" asked Superman.

Batman nodded. "The reason we can't find him is . . . he isn't here."

"We've already worked out that much," said The Flash.

"I didn't mean he's not in this apartment," Batman said, gazing out of the broken window. "Jason isn't in Gotham City. He might not even be on Earth."

# CHAPTER 2

# DEMONIC POSSESSION

**_VRUT·VRUT·VRUUUUT!_**

The Batboat sped quickly through an underground tunnel, causing waves to crash against the rocks. It followed a trail of lights lining the tunnel until a cave opened overhead. The Batboat floated up to a deck near a staircase leading up into the cavern.

**_SKREE! SKREE! SKREE! SKREE!_**

The Batboat's arrival upset the other occupants of the cave – a family of brown bats. They flapped their wings and retreated further into the shadows.

When the top of the boat opened, The Flash was the first one out. "Now *that* was a great ride! Not as fast as me, of course, but what is?" he bragged.

"Follow me," Batman said, climbing the staircase into his cave. "And keep up."

Without a word, Superman, Wonder Woman and The Flash trotted up the staircase behind him. At the top, they found Batman firing up the giant Batcomputer he used to monitor criminal activity. The powerful machine also served as the most high-tech crime lab in the world.

Batman put the wood sample from the chair on an instrument tray. The tray slid into the Batcomputer for analysis. As Superman and Wonder Woman waited for answers, The Flash wandered off to explore the rest of the Batcave.

"Look, but don't touch!" Batman growled without turning his attention away from the Batcomputer.

"How did you know I was going to?" asked The Flash. "Oh wait . . . World's Greatest Detective. Got it."

Taking in his surroundings, The Flash walked over to a row of display cases. Each one held uniforms for Batman and Robin, along with items the Dark Knight had collected from run-ins with past villains.

The Flash stopped in front of a display case that featured a wooden puppet dressed like a gangster. The Scarface puppet, with a mark across its face and a miniature tommy gun, had once belonged to the Ventriloquist. A few steps away, a case held the black mask of Bane, one of Batman's greatest and strongest enemies.

Also positioned around the cave were statues and props from past battles. A giant robot dinosaur loomed overhead and an oversized Joker playing card hung from the ceiling.

"This place reminds me of The Flash museum – except less fun," the Scarlet Speedster remarked. "I do like the giant penny though."

**BZZZRRT-ZRRT!**

An alarm from the Batcomputer signalled the analysis was complete. The monitor displayed the claw marks, along with the image of the monster that had made them. It had gnashing teeth, razor-sharp claws and golden metallic wings sprouting from its green uniform.

Superman winced. "A Parademon from Darkseid's army!" he said.

"Just what I feared," Batman said. "Kalibak was probably a distraction. While we battled him on the street, Parademons grabbed Jason from the apartment."

"But why?" asked Wonder Woman. "What reason would they have to take him?"

"If Darkseid has your friend, the reason can't be good," replied Superman.

"I guess this means we should pack our bags for a warmer climate," The Flash said, returning from his self-guided tour. He knew Darkseid ruled Apokolips. The planet was known for the unbearable heat from its blazing fire pits. It also was millions of kilometres away in deep space. "I hope you all have some frequent flier miles saved up. It's going to be a long trip."

"I've got something to shorten the distance," responded Batman.

Walking over to a rock wall, Batman removed a glove and placed his hand on an instrument panel. A blue light scanned his handprint, confirming his identity. Then a thick metal door opened a hidden vault.

"Don't touch anything!" warned Batman sternly, looking directly at The Flash. Then he put on his glove and entered the vault.

Shelves and cases lined the vault's walls. Most held locked containers, but one open box released an eerie green glow. The moment Superman passed it, he fell to his knees, gripping his stomach in pain. Batman's hand shot out, quickly closing the box's heavy lead lid.

"That's Kryptonite!" The Flash exclaimed.

"Why would you have that here?" asked Wonder Woman, rushing to help Superman back to his feet.

"It's . . . it's not his fault," Superman answered, trying to catch his breath. "I . . . I gave it to him. Just in case it needed to be used against me. If I . . . if I ever went bad."

"Darkseid once brainwashed Superman to control him to do whatever his evil mind desired," said Batman. "My fear is he might do the same to Jason."

"Is an antique collector really that powerful?" The Flash asked. Batman threw him a silent look, causing The Flash to regret his question.

Arriving at the final locked case, the Dark Knight opened it. He removed a small rectangular item similar to the one Kalibak used to disappear.

"Is that a cassette recorder? I think my dad had one of those old relics to play music," The Flash said with a grin.

"No," said Batman. "This is a Mother Box. It's a technology that can open a Boom Tube doorway. It will take us all the way to Apokolips to find Jason."

**_BWAAAAHHH! BWAAAAHHH!_**

Suddenly sirens blared, and the Batcave glowed with red lights. Exiting the vault, Batman ran towards the Batcomputer. The rest of the League followed behind.

"Computer, report!" commanded Batman.

"JUSTICE LEAGUE PRIORITY MESSAGE," the computer voice announced.

Up on the Batcomputer's main screen, a tall, green alien appeared. He had a large forehead, red eyes and wore a blue cape with red straps criss-crossing his body. It was J'onn J'onzz, the Martian Manhunter – one of the Justice League's most trusted members.

"J'onn, what's the problem?" Wonder Woman asked.

"Hello. This is a priority one emergency," reported Martian Manhunter.

"Who's causing trouble now?" asked The Flash.

"Everyone," said Manhunter. "There's been a rash of super-villain activity all at once. I'm sending you the Watchtower feed."

On the Batcomputer, a series of windows popped open. The first one showed Lex Luthor in ancient knight's armour attacking an armoured truck. As the security guards fired on him, the bullets bounced off harmlessly. *PING PING PINNGGG!*

The second window showed Felix Faust, a master of the dark arts. He used an ancient staff to raise an army of the undead.

A third window showed Sinestro, a former Green Lantern turned bad. He wore a special amulet around his neck to channel his power better than his own yellow ring. He directed his beam at a spaceship. **KRA-KOOM!**

Meanwhile, the fourth and final window showed Gorilla Grodd. The huge and highly intelligent gorilla wore a new helmet. He used it to control a group of humans with his mind.

"All of those items are magical relics from Jason's collection!" Batman exclaimed.

"It was only a matter of time before the rest of them ended up in the wrong hands," said Superman. "They must be stopped."

"The Watchtower can transport each of you to help capture them," offered Martian Manhunter.

"I'm afraid we can't, J'onn," replied Superman. "We already have a mission of vital importance on Apokolips – and we need to leave immediately!"

"Try contacting the other members of the Justice League," Wonder Woman offered. "They are your best hope while we're away."

"Very well. I shall see who else is available to help out. Good luck!" said Martian Manhunter. Then the Batcomputer's screen went black.

"All right then," Superman said. "Let's go and rescue Jason Blood!"

Batman activated the Mother Box, opening a circular Boom Tube doorway of bright light. The four members of the Justice League walked inside and disappeared.

*SHOOOM!*

# CHAPTER 3

# INTO THE PIT

**SHOOOM!**

On the planet Apokolips, the Boom Tube doorway reopened, and the Justice League walked out. The moment their feet touched the ground, they knew something felt wrong. Apokolips was known for its crushing heat. But the surrounding landscape was dark, stark and strangely unfamiliar.

"Are you sure this is the right place?" The Flash asked. "Or did we make a wrong turn somewhere?"

"The coordinates are never wrong," said Batman.

"This is definitely Apokolips – even if it doesn't appear to be," assured Superman.

The change in the environment was noticeable. The exhaust ports that vented the planet's fire pits were dark – like the pits themselves had gone out. And the heavy smell of sulphur normally in the air was oddly absent. Most surprising, the air temperature was low – even cold.

"I never thought I'd say this, but . . . I'm kind of cold. Not a Captain Cold kind of cold. But still . . . *brrrrrr!*" said The Flash, rubbing his arms to stay warm.

"There's definitely a harsh chill in the air," agreed Wonder Woman.

Already thinking strategy, the Dark Knight scanned the horizon to devise a plan. "We can cover more ground if we split up."

"I wouldn't advise it. I've dealt with Darkseid before, and Apokolips is extremely dangerous," warned Superman. "Darkseid has an unlimited army of Parademons that patrol the skies and ground. We'll be picked off one by one if we separate."

"He has a point," said Wonder Woman. "For now, we're stronger if we stay together."

"For now," repeated Batman.

"Did anybody bring a torch?" asked The Flash. "It's dark without the fire pits. I don't want to step in something gross."

"It's better if we search in the dark. We won't be found that way. Unless someone is against that too," answered Batman, walking away from the group.

"Was it something I said?" asked The Flash.

"He's just concerned for his friend. We all are," replied Wonder Woman.

The team walked silently through the ruins of Apokolips, searching for signs of Jason Blood. Giant stone statues, originally built in Darkseid's image, were crumbling. Broken stones were scattered across the ground. Even the skies, normally filled with flying Parademons, showed no signs of life.

Sifting through the rubble of a nearby building, Batman looked for a clue -- any clue – pointing to the whereabouts of Jason Blood. The Flash cautiously approached to cheer him up.

"It's like trying to find hay in a needle stack," said The Flash with a smile. "Am I right?" Batman didn't respond.

"Um . . . you know I could scour the entire planet in two hours tops," offered The Flash.

"That would be a bad mistake," Batman replied. "Right now, we have the element of surprise. Darkseid doesn't know we're here. We can use that to our advantage. Your running will only draw attention."

"Spoilsport," replied The Flash.

"Besides, my Mother Box is able to detect the heat signature from other Boom Tube devices. From what I can tell, this is the area where Kalibak returned. We must be close," guessed Batman, looking at the read-out on his device.

While Batman collected a rock sample to add to his Utility Belt, Superman flew into the air. He hovered above the ruins to get a better view of the planet's dark landscape. Meanwhile, Wonder Woman used her Amazonian strength to lift and search under some fallen stone pillars.

Unsure how to help, The Flash sat on top of the toppled head of a Darkseid statue.

"Who knew Darkseid would make such a great chair?" The Flash said. Then he noticed a pinpoint of light shining up through the cracks of a nearby pile of rubble. "Hey . . . I think I found something! Look at this!"

The Flash walked over to the small mound of stones. As he sifted through the rubble, more light escaped. Superman glided down and Wonder Woman jogged over to see if they could help. But Batman backed away.

"Wait," shouted the Dark Knight. "Don't touch it – !"

Suddenly the ground cracked open, and a burst of light encased the Justice League. Unable to resist the force field, the team plunged into the ground. A long narrow shaft deposited them on a concrete floor.

## THOOOM!

"When someone tells you not to touch something, don't touch it!" yelled Batman.

They stood in the darkness. The only light came through the narrow shaft above them.

Batman studied its distance. "It's too high for my grapnel to reach. Do you think it's wide enough to carry anyone through, Wonder Woman?"

Before the Amazonian warrior could respond, a voice came from the shadows.

"You know what they say about curiosity and the cat," the voice said. "I really think they meant . . . *bat*."

## HA HA HA HA HA!

A low cackle of laughter pierced the darkness. Then a portly old woman stepped into the light.

The woman had high arching eyebrows and a thick head of white hair. A sickly yellow cape hung off her drab green clothing, and her black nailed fingers clutched a blunt golden energy rod. Granny Goodness, the evil aid to Darkseid, allowed a crooked smile to cut across her wrinkled face.

Batman lunged forward, his cape billowing behind him. Just before he could tackle her, Granny Goodness raised her energy rod.

**KRACKLE!**

The photon blast dropped Batman to the ground with a **THUD!** Granny's energy rod sparked as she pointed it towards the rest of the team.

"That was a warning shot, my lowlies. Granny gives you only one."

"Where's Jason Blood?" barked Batman, clutching his stomach in pain.

Granny Goodness placed her hand on her chest, as if insulted. "That's rather forward of you. Granny Goodness will answer your question, but only after you escape from the X-Pit – if you're lucky."

The room around them lit up, revealing a stark arena. The gashed dirt floor showed the damage from past battles. High stone walls surrounded them on all sides, stretching far out of reach. Large balconies hung over the top of the walls, providing plenty of seating for spectators to watch the performers.

"Welcome to my training ground," said Granny Goodness. "Today, this maze of dangerous obstacles and traps will be an arena. You will perform for the pleasure of the Almighty Darkseid."

"And where is your master?" asked Superman. "Where is Darkseid?"

"Where I always am, Son of Krypton," a voice boomed. It came from a huge figure looking down from a balcony. "Above you."

Darkseid was a formidable titan with grey, stone-like skin. He had jagged cracks along his forehead and a protruding brow. His blue uniform stretched across his wide chest. Darkseid was Superman's ultimate enemy. The Man of Steel clenched his fists and flew up to meet the super-villain head on.

"Why did you kidnap Jason Blood?" yelled Superman.

"The power he contains is of great use to me. And soon, when I am through with him, he will be no more," answered Darkseid bluntly. Then he lowered his head towards Superman and his eyes glowed red.

## KRA·KOOM!

A pair of Omega Beams, fired directly from Darkseid's eyes, shot Superman out of the air. Crackling with energy, the Man of Steel crashed to the concrete floor. His body created a crater upon impact.

"I have always admired your tenacity, Superman," said Darkseid with a wicked smile. "Even if you harbour a fool's hope."

"It is foolish to confront your benefactor!" Granny Goodness taunted as the Man of Steel picked himself up. "It would be best to save your energy. You will need it if you are to survive the X-Pit."

Granny Goodness pushed a button on her energy rod to encase the Justice League in another force field. She then lowered them through an opening in the floor and into the X-Pit.

From a monitor screen in their balcony, Granny Goodness and Darkseid watched the team float down. Then she pressed the button on her energy rod again, releasing the Justice League from the force field. Dropping the last metre to the X-Pit's floor, they found themselves inside a sealed room.

"Let's see how they handle this." Granny Goodness laughed and then activated a lever on the monitor's control panel.

**SKREEEECH!** Without warning, the room's walls closed in around the Justice League. Superman and Wonder Woman rushed towards them, pressing their arms and bodies against them. Surprisingly, their considerable strength did nothing to stop the walls from closing in.

"Search for an exit!" yelled Batman.

"I can't see any," answered Superman.

"Search harder!" replied Batman.

Up in the balcony, Granny Goodness turned another switch on the monitor's control panel. "Let's help these lowlies find what they're looking for," she said.

**SKREECH!**

In the X-Pit, a trapdoor in the floor opened to reveal a small circular grate. The grate's metal bars were too close together to slide between, so Superman grabbed them to pull them apart. The instant his hands gripped the bars, a surge of electricity coursed through his body. The Man of Steel fell backwards in pain.

"Stand aside!" shouted Wonder Woman, stepping forward. She removed the golden rope from her belt and lassoed the metal bars. She pulled with all of her Amazonian strength.

In a shower of sparks, the grate ripped free of the floor. Without a moment to lose, the Justice League plunged into the hole before the walls came crashing in on them.

"Out of the frying pan and into the laser fire." Granny Goodness cackled as she watched the action unfold on the monitor. Darkseid allowed himself to smile as Granny Goodness pressed a number of knobs on the control panel with both hands.

On the screen, the Justice League slid down a tunnel and dropped into another enclosed room. Guns appeared from the walls and began firing lasers.

### PEECHOO PEECHOO!

Superman used his own laser vision to try to destroy the guns. But as soon as one gun exploded, a new one replaced it.

"I can't shoot them fast enough," shouted the Man of Steel.

"Let me try," answered Batman.

The Dark Knight pulled three Batarangs from his Utility Belt and threw them at multiple guns. But the lasers destroyed each Batarang before it ever found its target.

Once again, Wonder Woman came to the rescue. She used her bracelets to deflect several laser beams into a wall. The concentrated laser fire exploded, opening a hole in the concrete. The Justice League jumped through it. To their surprise, they found a staircase leading to the surface. They had escaped the X-Pit.

"AAARRGGHHHH!" Granny Goodness shouted as she watched the Justice League disappear from her screen. "How could they escape?"

In frustration, she shot a photon blast with her energy rod, destroying the monitor. Realizing what she had done, Granny Goodness kneeled before her master.

"Rise," commanded Darkseid. "Let us deal with the prisoner."

Granny Goodness followed Darkseid down a long, winding tunnel and into a large dungeon. Jason Blood, chained to the dungeon wall, hung before them. His brown suit and black shirt looked dirty and wrinkled. His red chestnut hair had a streak of white down its centre, betraying the fact that he was much older than he appeared.

"I beg you, Mighty Darkseid, let me fetch my war dogs. Granny can still hunt down and punish the Justice League."

"I will not allow it," boomed Darkseid. "Not when I can unleash my own hunter!"

Darkseid chanted, *"Gone, gone, the form of man, arise MY demon, ETRIGAN!"*

Jason's eyes lit up with flames!

Jason Blood's body arched as Etrigan the Demon detached from it to take physical form. Etrigan had yellow skin, orange eyes, winged ears and horns on his head. He ran his blunt claws over his red uniform and adjusted his tattered cape. With the curse magically lifted, the Demon knelt on one knee before Darkseid.

"What do you wish of me, my master?" asked Etrigan.

Darkseid smiled. "Capture the Justice League and bring them to me."

Etrigan bowed. "I am here to serve," he said. Then he leaped out of the room.

# CHAPTER 4

# DEMONS UNLEASHED

On the surface of Apokolips, the Justice League watched the horizon as an army of Parademons flew towards them. The staircase from the X-Pit had brought them to a ruined city on the surface. Now hiding among the rubble of destroyed buildings, they listened as the Parademons grunted and gnashed their teeth overhead.

"We're going to be seen," worried The Flash, crouching next to a rock.

"Quiet!" whispered Wonder Woman, hiding across from him.

"We need to find Darkseid's fortress," said Batman. "That's our best chance of finding Jason."

"It's the tallest structure on Apokolips," said Superman. "It won't be hard to miss."

Suddenly, a Parademon's clawed feet landed on the ground next to Batman. **SNARL! GRONKK!** Immediately it bleated out a cry, alerting the rest of its patrol.

"I told you we'd be found!" The Flash said.

"We can't stay here any longer," Wonder Woman shouted, knocking out the snarling Parademon with a punch. "Run!"

The rest of the Parademons swarmed to the ground, their wings buzzing angrily as they surrounded the team. With too many to outrun, they'd have to fight their way through them.

"Someone should call pest control," warned The Flash, avoiding the slashing claws of a nearby Parademon.

"I'll get right on it," said Superman, using his eyes to fire laser beams at a Parademon lunging towards him.

**ROOOOARR!**

A fireball struck Superman by surprise, knocking him to the ground. He looked up to see the swarm of Parademons part before him. Etrigan the Demon walked through them, clearly in charge of this patrol.

"Etrigan! Stop now! We are not your enemies," Batman said, stepping out from behind a broken wall. "I'm Jason's friend."

"I am no longer Jason's prisoner," stated Etrigan. "Let his body rot in that dungeon. I only serve my master, Darkseid."

Etrigan released a wall of flame so intense it singed Batman's cape. Superman quickly stepped in front of the Dark Knight. He used his super breath to force back the flames.

As Batman looked over his shoulder for an escape route, a tall spire in the distance caught his eye.

"Darkseid's fortress is over there!" he shouted, pointing towards the large stone tower many kilometres away.

"Let's go and find Jason while Superman holds off Etrigan," Wonder Woman shouted. She leaped and flew towards the tower.

"But it's too far away for me to reach quickly on foot," Batman replied

"I've got your back – or should I say, you've got mine," said The Flash. Then he turned his back to the Dark Knight.

"What are you doing?" asked Batman.

"What does it look like? Hop on and I'll carry you," said The Flash.

"You can't be serious," Batman growled.

"Unless you can run faster than the speed of light, then my way is much better," said The Flash.

Batman frowned but climbed on The Flash's back. In an instant, they dashed towards the fortress in a blur.

Superman exhausted his air supply, and Etrigan's fire breath overtook him. The Man of Steel tumbled backwards down a hill, crashing into another statue of Darkseid.

"Give up," snarled Etrigan. "You are outnumbered and can't possibly stop us all."

"That won't prevent me from trying," replied Superman.

The Man of Steel jabbed his fingers deep into the stone statue and hurled it towards Etrigan. **BOOOM!** The statue crashed to the ground, throwing up a huge cloud of debris. Superman used the distraction to spring into the sky and fly towards the fortress.

Moments later, Etrigan emerged from the dust, shaking dirt from his tattered cape. He bounded towards the fortress in pursuit of the Justice League.

***

"So . . . I'm not noticing a doorbell," said The Flash. "Do we just knock?"

Wonder Woman, The Flash and Batman had arrived at Darkseid's fortress. Its giant stone tower loomed above them. They had crossed a moat of cooling molten rock and now stood in front of two huge granite doors.

Wonder Woman pressed her fingers between the doors, trying to pry them open. They wouldn't budge.

"Let me try," said a voice from above. Superman swooped down to rejoin his friends.

Focusing his heat vision, Superman turned the doors bright red, and they began to melt. When a large hole opened, the team stepped through it into the fortress' entry hall. Not wasting a moment, they crossed the hall and burst into Darkseid's throne room.

A long, torn carpet stretched before them, leading up a pair of steps to a stone throne. But behind it, looking out of an open window, stood Darkseid.

"DARKSEID!" shouted Superman. "We're here for Jason Blood!"

"So am I, Son of Krypton," Darkseid said, turning to gaze upon the heroes. His stone face had a look of sadness. "Apokolips, my planet, . . . is dying. Its fires have nearly gone out. Soon the planet will crumble without its heat source. But I've found another."

"Etrigon!" Batman exclaimed. "You're planning to use the Demon to relight this planet's core."

"Not if we have something to say about it," added Wonder Woman.

"You're too late," announced Darkseid. "It has already begun."

Batman had heard enough. With a flick of his wrist, the Dark Knight sent two Batarangs straight towards Darkseid. But the super-villain simply swatted them aside with a wave of his hand.

When Superman and Wonder Woman flew towards him to attack, Darkseid's eyes glowed red. Thin Omega Beams split in a zigzagging pattern, striking both of them. They tumbled backwards, skidding across the stone floor.

Then The Flash sped forward and landed a rapid series of punches to the super-villain's midsection. Darkseid smiled, unaffected. Then he kicked the speedster, sending him skidding into his friends.

"None of you are of concern to me. Leave now, and I will allow you all to suffer back on your own world," promised Darkseid.

"Never!" said the Man of Steel, standing back up.

"I used to look forward to our battles," Darkseid said. "It's a shame really."

With one giant blast, Darkseid's wide Omega Beam filled the room with a bright red light. When it struck the Justice League, they disappeared.

At that moment, Etrigan dashed into the throne room. "Where have they gone, my master?"

"Teleported to the core," said Darkseid, turning towards a flight of steps leading beneath the fortress. "Come. It's time to reignite the fires of Apokolips!"

# CHAPTER 5

# DEALING WITH
# THE DEVIL

Deep within Apokolips, the Justice League sat in chains within the planet's cavernous central core. Darkseid, with Kalibak and Granny Goodness at his side, had sent the heroes here to witness the planet's rebirth.

"Look around you," the super-villain said, gesturing towards the barely glowing bed of lava before them. "This is all that remains of the lifeblood of Apokolips. Once vibrant, it has now cooled. Its flame struggles to avoid being extinguished."

"Maybe it should burn out," said Superman. A vice fastened to his eyes prevented him from using his heat vision.

**KRACKLE!**

"Quiet your tongue," barked Granny, shocking Superman with her energy rod.

"Through my kindness," said Darkseid, "I allow you to witness this planet's rebirth."

Etrigan then entered the cavern. He carried a frail old man who had a familiar tuft of white hair running down the middle of his head. Etrigan dumped the man on the ground next to the Justice League.

Unable to see, Superman could only sit and listen. Shifting her arms and body, Wonder Woman struggled with her chains. Even The Flash couldn't wriggle free. Batman sat silently, observing the room.

"If we can't stop him," said Batman, "no one will."

"Don't give up hope, my friend," said the old man. Then he offered a faint smile and dropped a lock pick near Batman's hand.

"Jason?" asked Batman.

The old man struggled to his feet. He shuffled towards Darkseid.

"Sit down, my brother," said Etrigan, stomping his foot down in front of Jason to block his path. "This is not your place."

Darkseid held up his hand. "Allow him to speak, Etrigan."

Jason took a deep breath. "I beg you, Darkseid, release your hold on Etrigan. The Demon's full power is unstable. It could send the core into a meltdown that would destroy your entire planet."

"I am counting on that power to help make Apokolips strong again," argued Darkseid. "It's a risk worth taking."

Darkseid turned to the Demon. "Etrigan, I command you to breathe fire into the lava core. Ignite it and begin our rebirth!"

**RRRROOOOOAR!**

Etrigan released a hot blast of fire into the core. The bed of lava bubbled alive and a sea of flames arose.

"It's working," proclaimed Darkseid. "Breathe your power into it once more."

Before Etrigan could fire off another blast, a long, deep **RUUMMBBLE** shook the floor of the cavern.

"The core can't take another blast like that," warned Batman. "We're sitting on a ticking time bomb here."

"What can we do?" wondered The Flash.

"I'm working on that," said Batman, wriggling his wrist with the lock pick.

Darkseid stood in front of the boiling lava, looking down with pride. "Once Apokolips is reborn, I shall use my Demon to become the sole power in the universe."

Etrigan scrunched his nose with confusion. "If I contain such power, then why do I need you?" he said. "What if I wish to rule the galaxy by myself? Or even to destroy it?"

"Nonsense, Etrigan. Use your full power to breathe into the core," commanded Darkseid, pointing towards the lava. "Serve your master by lighting its eternal flame."

Etrigan shook his head. Sensing his rebellion, Darkseid's eyes began to glow. "Demon, do as I command!"

"I will not be forced," spat Etrigan. "I am free of the curse that bound me and free of your control. All that matters is what I want – which is to destroy everything."

"You dare defy me?" asked Darkseid. He swung his fist towards Etrigan's head.

**KRAK·THOOM!**

Etrigan stopped Darkseid's fist in his clawed grip and returned the punch instead. It struck Darkseid across the jaw, knocking him to the ground.

"You rude beast. Parademons *attack*!" cried Darkseid.

A group of Parademons flew down the stone staircase and into the cavern. They swarmed Etrigan, only to be met with a ferocious blast of his fiery breath. They scattered and fled up the stairs for safety.

During the commotion, Batman unlocked his chains and freed his friends. Then he unleashed an array of exploding Batarangs above the staircase.

*THOOOM!* An avalanche of rocks rained down on the passageway. Superman then used his cold breath to freeze the rocks solid and prevent any more Parademons from entering the cavern.

Meanwhile, The Flash ran circles around Granny Goodness. *KRACKLE! KRACKLE! KRACKLE!* She fired her energy rod over and over, missing the speedster each time. Using the distraction, Wonder Woman threw her lasso around Granny to bind her up tight.

Near the lava bed, Darkseid and Etrigan continued to trade blows. Unable to stand idly by any longer, Kalibak leaped towards the pair with his magical sword.

"Get your hands off him, or face my wrath!" he warned.

**KLONG!** The flat side of Kalibak's blade bounced off Etrigan's head. As the Demon fell to one knee, Kalibak turned to Darkseid. "I did it, father!" he cried. "I saved you!"

**SPLUGE!** Etrigan belched an enormous fireball at Kalibak. The impact dislodged the sword from Kulibak's hands and knocked the villain through the cavern's roof.

"But who saves you, son?" wondered Darkseid in disgust.

Weak but determined, Jason staggered towards Darkseid. "There's only one chance to stop this," he pleaded. "You must release Etrigan, or this planet will be destroyed!"

Darkseid stared him down with cold, uncaring eyes.

"Are you truly prepared to sacrifice this planet?" asked Jason.

**RUUMMMBLE!**

The ground shook once more and huge chunks of the cavern's roof crashed to the floor. The violent quake seemed to shake Darkseid from a trance.

"Very well," he whispered reluctantly. "I . . . release you."

"NO! Do it properly," Jason pleaded. "Speak the sacred words!"

Darkseid's stone face twisted with a grimace. *"Gone, gone O Etrigan! Rise once more the form of man!"*

Etrigan tried to fight against Darkseid's magical command. His body shook and his claws grasped for the super-villain. But his hands faded and he was unable to grab him.

The Demon's spirit returned to Jason Blood's body. The two cursed souls merged into one. Jason fell to the ground, clutching his chest.

"Welcome home," Jason said to himself, struggling to stand. Then he recited a magic spell. "KOR GOTH RECTI CHAR UUN DRAGA!"

The lava settled down to a simmer, stopping the core from complete meltdown. When he finished speaking, Jason fell backwards into Batman's arms.

"You lost, Darkseid," said Superman.

"Have I?" asked Darkseid. "Look around, Superman. The flames of Apokolips burn bright once more. My planet is reborn. Ruling the rest of the universe can wait."

"Victorious even in defeat," said Batman.

The Caped Crusader passed Jason's unconscious body to Wonder Woman. Then he bent down to pick up Excalibur.

Darkseid turned to leave. He smiled, sensing the anger boiling up in Superman.

"It's not that easy," said Superman. "This isn't over, Darkseid!"

"You're right, Son of Krypton. It's only over for now," the super-villain said, waving his hand in a mocking gesture. "Now return to Earth, and go with my blessing."

Disgusted, Superman balled up his fists, preparing to strike. But The Flash stepped forward and placed a hand on the Man of Steel's arm to stop him. Superman paused and looked back at Wonder Woman cradling the elderly Jason in her arms. It was enough to remind him that they needed to get Jason back home to recover.

Not wasting a moment, Wonder Woman released Granny Goodness from her lasso, and Batman opened a Boom Tube. Together the Justice League entered the doorway of light, leaving Apokolips behind.

**SHOOOM!**

***

Jason Blood opened his eyes. Seated again in his armchair, he'd regained his more youthful appearance.

He glanced around the room. Picture frames had been restored. The broken window overlooking the city was replaced. And most importantly, all of his lost artefacts had been recovered thanks to the Justice League. Jason leaned back in his chair, letting out a laboured sigh.

"Was it all a dream?" he asked.

"No . . . a nightmare," answered a familiar voice. "And a very real one at that."

Batman stepped from behind Jason's chair, placing a hand on his shoulder. "I'm sorry you have to live with your curse again."

"Oh, well," said Jason wistfully. "I wouldn't be the same without Etrigan, and I would hate to ponder the alternative. Nevertheless, thank you for helping set things right, old friend."

"And thank you for not destroying the universe," said The Flash with a smirk. "We kinda like it here."

The rest of the League joined him in laughter.

⟨ END ⟩

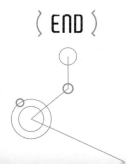

⟨ **TARGET: AT LARGE** ⟩

# DARKSEID

Worshipped as a god, Darkseid rules the planet Apokolips with an iron fist. His power comes from the Omega Effect, which he can focus in the form of Omega Beams he shoots from his eyes. Darkseid also possesses super-strength and invulnerability, and he can control his victims with his mind. At one time, he was even able to brainwash Superman into doing his evil bidding. As one of the most powerful beings in existence, Darkseid is the greatest threat to the Justice League . . . and to the universe!

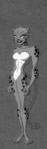

LEX LUTHOR     THE JOKER     CHEETAH     SINESTRO     CAPTAIN COLD

BLACK MANTA

AMAZO

GORILLA GRODD

STAR SAPPHIRE

BRAINIAC

DARKSEID

HARLEY QUINN

BIZARRO

THE SHADE

MONGUL

POISON IVY

MR. FREEZE

COPPERHEAD

ULTRA-
HUMANITE

CAPTAIN
BOOMERANG

SOLOMON GRUNDY

BLACK ADAM

DEADSHOT

CIRCE

CLOCK KING

SCARECROW

MANHUNTER

KILLER FROST

GIGANTA

PROFESSOR
ZOOM

KILLER CROC

TWO-FACE

METALLO

DR. DESTINY

KALIBAK

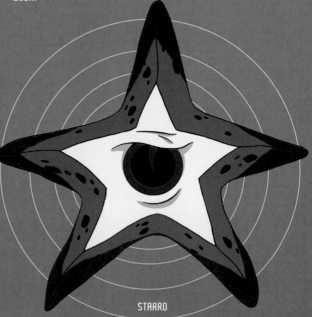

STARRO

# STRENGTH IN NUMBERS

AMAZO AND THE PLANETARY ACROUT
by Brandon T. Snider & Tim Levins

DARKSEID AND THE FIRES OF APOKOLIPS
by Derek Fridolfs & Tim Levins

INJUSTICE GANG AND THE DEADLY NIGHTSHADE
by Derek Fridolfs & Tim Levins

STARRO AND THE CYBERSPORE
by Brandon T. Snider & Tim Levins

⟨ raintree ⟩

a Capstone company — publishers for children

# GLOSSARY

**analysis** careful study of something

**artefact** object made by human beings, especially a tool or weapon used in the past

**benefactor** someone who gives a gift or a benefit to someone else

**brainwash** make someone believe something by saying it repeatedly

**climate** the usual weather that occurs in a place

**coordinate** one of a set of numbers used to show the position of a point on a map or graph

**cylindrical** having a shape with flat, circular ends and sides shaped like the outside of a tube

**moat** deep, wide ditch dug all around a castle or fort that is typically filled with water to prevent attacks

**priority** something that is more important or urgent than other things

**strategy** careful plan or method

**sulphur** yellow chemical used in gunpowder, matches and fertilizer that smells like rotten eggs

**transform** change form or shape

# THINK

1. Do you think Batman should have the chunk of Kryptonite he keeps in the Batcave? Explain why you agree or disagree.

2. Why does Etrigan disobey Darkseid's commands to reignite Apokolips' core? Was he right to do so?

3. The Justice League let Darkseid get away at the end of the story. Should they have done this? Explain your answers.

# WRITE

1. The Justice League decides to rescue Jason Blood instead of staying on Earth to recover the stolen artefacts. Write about a time when you had to make a difficult choice. Describe how it worked out.

2. Batman stores souvenirs from his adventures in the Batcave. If you had a secret headquarters, what would you store in it? Make a list and draw a picture of the most important item.

3. What does Darkseid do after the Justice League returns to Earth? Write a short story about his next evil plot to take over the universe!

## AUTHOR

**DEREK FRIDOLFS** is the bestselling writer of the DC Secret Hero Society series, and the Eisner Award-nominated co-writer of *Batman Li'l Gotham*. He has worked in comics for more than 15 years as a writer, artist and inker on *Adventures of Superman*, *Detective Comics*, *Arkham City Endgame*, *Sensational Comics Featuring Wonder Woman*, *Justice League Beyond*, *Teen Titans Go*, *Scooby-Doo*, *Looney Tunes*, *Teenage Mutant Ninja Turtles*, *Dexter's Laboratory*, *Clarence*, *Regular Show* and *Adventure Time*. He resides in California, USA.

## ILLUSTRATOR

**TIM LEVINS** is best known for his work on the Eisner Award-winning DC Comics series *Batman: Gotham Adventures*. Tim has illustrated other DC titles, such as *Justice League Adventures*, *Batgirl*, *Metal Men* and *Scooby-Doo*, and has also done work for Marvel Comics and Archie Comics. Tim enjoys life in Ontario, Canada, with his wife, son, dog and two horses.